This Is Mohan

By Ella Grove

Artist: Edith Burkholder

Rod and Staff Publishers, Inc.
P.O. Box 3, Hwy. 172
Crockett, Kentucky 41413
Telephone (606) 522-4348

Printed in U.S.A.

ISBN 0-7399-0034-X
Catalog no. 2437

8 9 10 11 12 — 15 14 13 12 11 10 09 08 07 06

THIS IS MOHAN

He was one.

Then he was two.

By Ella Grove

Now he is three.

He does not live in Canada;
Nor in the U.S.A.
He does not live in Mexico,
But very far away.

He's in a land called India,
Where children run and play;

And watch the monkeys frisk around
At closing of the day.

Mohan's house is not made of brick;
It is not made of stone;
Its walls are mud; the roof above
Is made of leaves of palm.

Father mixed the mud with his feet,
Put water in every batch.

He placed the palm leaves in neat rows,
And called the roof a thatch.

His hair is black; his skin is brown;
His teeth are snowy white.
He cuts a stick from a neemwood tree
And chews with all his might . . .

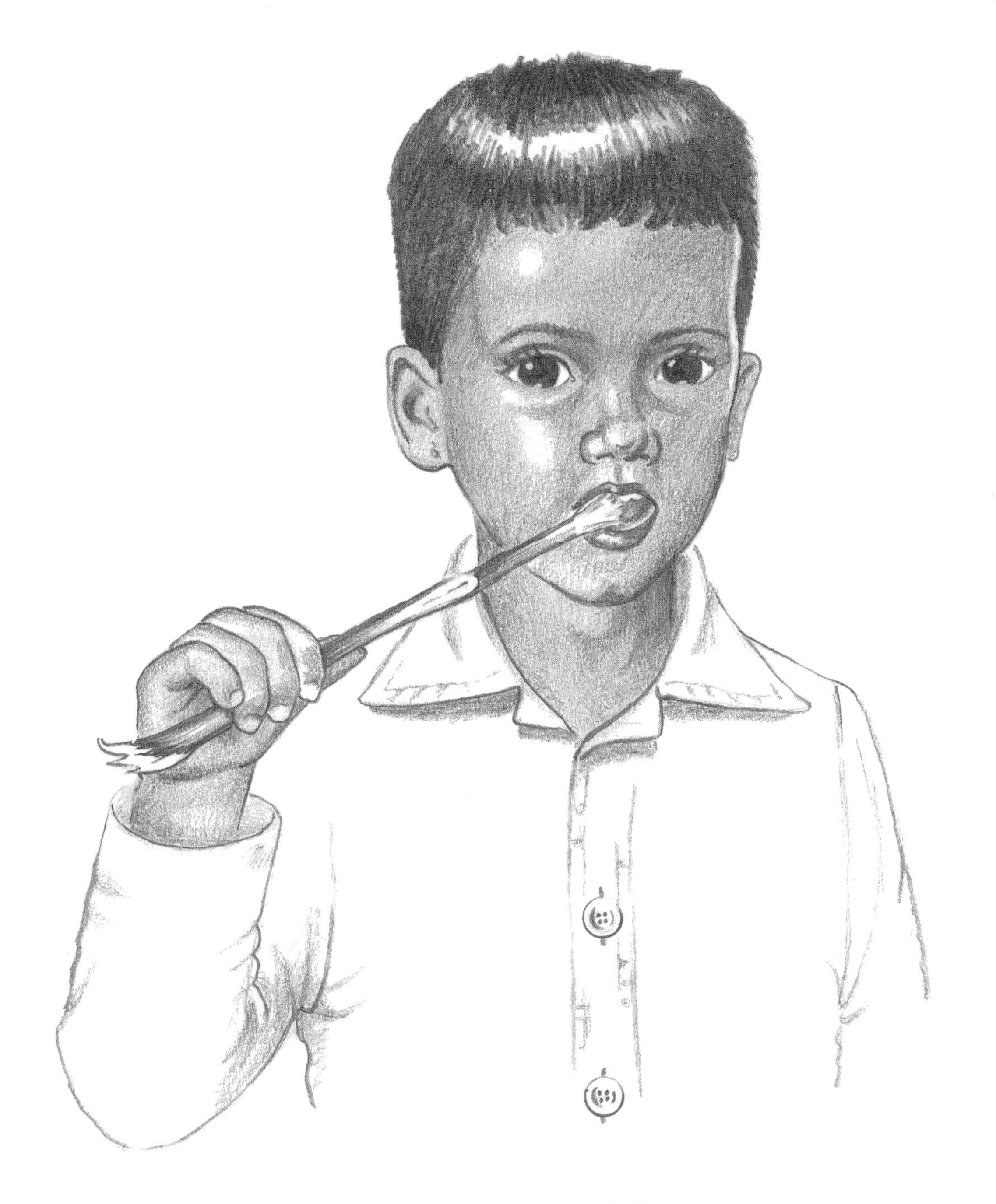

Until one end is shredded fine—
It makes a splendid brush;
He scrubs his teeth until they shine,
Like Indian children must.

He does not want at all to cry;
He does not want to pout;
He always wears a nice big smile
When folks are all about.

He likes to sing a happy song
Of birds and flowers and trees;

He plays with baby goats and lambs,
And holds them on his knees.

Our Mohan has some little toys;
They're not like yours at all.
He does not have a car or truck;
He does not have a ball.

He does not have a game or train;
He does not have a book.
He has a hoop to push around
With stick and wire hook.

He eats his meals from a small bowl
While seated on the floor;
With dash of spice, he eats his rice,
Holds up his bowl for more.

He always has rice for breakfast,
For lunch and supper, too;
He does not grumble one small bit,
'Cause rice is good for you.

He does not have a great big bed;
He does not have a cot.
But when he is a sleepy head,
He goes right to a spot . . .

Gets out a mat his mother made,
And spreads it on the floor.
His blanket covers head and all,
While angels watch him o'er.

One day a Christian family came
Who had a little boy,
And he became small Mohan's friend,
Which filled his heart with joy.

He took our Mohan by the hand;
They went to Sunday school;
He learned about the Word of God;
He learned the Golden Rule.

And then the children all stood up,
They made a long straight row;
They sang a little song that said,
"Jesus loves me, this I know."

Our Mohan really liked the words,
"The Bible tells me so."
Then off he ran, right to his home;
His parents, too, should know.